SCION

Book III

House of the Twelfth Planet

By

Miriam Newman

DCL Publications, LLC

DCL Publications, LLC

First Edition March 2020

DCL Publications
1033 Plymouth Dr.
Grafton, OH 44044

ISBN 978-1-7328475-8-3

Cover design by Lynn Hubbard

Model: ©curaphotography - Can Stock Photo Inc.

PUBLISHED IN THE UNITED STATES OF AMERICA

Chapter One

Her last memory was of sleeping in Caius's arms. Her first was of his face.

There were other faces, too—human faces unlike her Thelonian Lord's. More like her own. Shrill beeping noises. Nearly unbearable lights and a cold, sharp smell.

"Just be patient a moment," one of the human faces said. "We will have you out shortly."

Out of where, Lela thought, but she could see hands and feel them on her, too. Strange sensations, not unpleasant, but…invading. Removing things from her skin. Through it all, Caius's steady, calm voice kept her from utter panic.

"You are awakening from a long sleep," he told her, and she could well believe it. How long could you sleep, to forget where you were and why?

"You are on board a space transport," he told her. "I have been with you the whole time. Just let the crew help you."

She lay still, hardly daring to blink.

"There," a woman's voice said cheerily. "All finished now. How do you feel?"

Lela's stare fixed on her. A medico. Fully human, understandable, not a threat. Dimly, she remembered. This woman had given her a substance that made her sleep, with Caius in their tiny cabin accommodation. His heartbeat was the last thing she had felt before she slept. Now she was inside one of the sleeping pods she had seen the crew members use. They had gone into the long sleep, and so had she. There were others, around her, stirring and stepping out of their pods.

"Strange," she told the medico, then looked past her to Caius. "How long have I slept?"

"Twelve years by our suns. But now we are coming into the orbit of Colony Twelve, where I believe the days and years are somewhat longer."

She shook her head. She was a simple nonni-girl from Danaali, a farmer, not a learned person who would know such things. It was all very well for Caius to tell her. He had a law-giver's degree. She was confused except for one thing: on Colony 12 she was no longer a slave.

"Can I sit up?" she asked cautiously.

"Of course." The medico whose name she

now remembered—Jorelle—swung back the remaining lid on the pod, freeing her lower body. "Just go slowly. You may be dizzy."

She was—both dizzy and cold. Released from the confines of the sheltering pod and dressed in only a thin silver gown, she began to shudder.

"I need some clothes."

"I know." Caius, dressed in a tunic and pants, presumably had been wakened before her. He turned to take one of the silver blankets they used on the transport from a tall metal case near the pods and bent to wrap it around her.

"Here," he said, tucking it. "Let me do it." Sliding an arm behind her back and another under her knees, he lifted her from the pod over Jorelle's immediate protest.

"She should remain here to be

monitored."

"No." He might be a passenger on a mercenary ship, but Caius was a Lord of Rank—or at least he had been. He was not accustomed to being opposed. "She will recover faster where she feels safe than she will here, where she does not."

"She is precious cargo," Jorelle tried once again, but Caius started walking.

"I know."

Gratefully, Lela cushioned her face against his shoulder, knowing his strength. If he wanted to take her somewhere, he would, and just then she was grateful, anxious to be away from the medical bay. No one would stop him and she wanted to go with him. She hadn't always, but that seemed long ago.

The lights were not so bright in the hallways where moving floors took them in the direction Caius apparently wanted to go. She let herself relax and close her eyes, remembering that he knew how the ship worked. They were going to a free place...she remembered now. One where he would no longer be her Lord, but he was still acting like he was and she made no objection.

Apparently she had fallen asleep again, because she roused when they entered the cabin they had been given. Yes, this was familiar, too, even to the annoying beep of the sliding door that let them in. She had always been afraid it would close too soon and pin her though he assured her it would not. It was a plain chamber but equipped with everything necessary including a spacious sleeping platform in an alcove formed by walls of a hard substance she still didn't understand.

It didn't matter. The platform was warm

and supportive and he slid her in close to the wall before lying down on the other side. His presence between her and the door gave her instinctive comfort and she was waking fully. She remembered now why she craved that protection. Sighing, she turned and put her face against him.

"Better now?" he asked, stroking her hair. She had been sold many times for that hair, blue-black and shining, and for her fair skin and blue eyes that were so rare on the planet Thelona. But thank the gods she was there no longer. She nodded, without words.

"In a while I will get you something to drink. You should take only liquids for a day or two until your body is ready for food again. We will not be landing right away. You'll have time to be ready."

"What will it be like?" she whispered. At

that moment, she felt entirely at peace and had no wish to disturb it. But they had not endured a journey of twelve years for nothing. Twelve years to reach Colony Twelve. Perhaps it was an omen. Caius had warned her people there did not believe in omens or in gods, though. She might be the only one who did.

"I'm not sure," he admitted, "but they know we are coming. I have requested asylum and they have given us permission to land."

Why should they not, she wondered? He was a Lord of Rank, a law-speaker, a judge, a man who had fought for eight years with the Mercenary Corps. And he was wealthy— wealthy enough to have bought her and much else besides. They were hardly beggars.

"Both of us?" she asked.

He chuckled. Caius was not prone to laughter, so she knew she had really amused him this time.

"Yes, both of us."

She was silent for a moment, but not unthinking. "What did Jorelle mean, that I am precious cargo?"

Caius's arm tightened around her.

"That you are important to me, I suppose. And you are."

Again she was silent, processing his answer. It was pleasing, but there was something more. Her memories were coming back. The crew, even Jorelle, had watched them as if puzzled by their odd pairing—a Thelonian man with a human woman. Would they now? Or was it her hesitancy, her uncertainty in the face of anything complicated that made them watch? Those things she could learn. But she could not change the fact that she and Caius were different.

"They are Earthers on Twelve?" she questioned.

Caius nodded. "Mostly."

The crew was comprised mainly of Earthers, too. They were the ones who had looked hard at her, though they had been unfailingly polite. So she didn't ask Caius what they would be like.

Chapter Two

Roger Lankford, Governor of Colony Twelve's first and as yet only settlement, was having an interesting morning.

"Transport coming in," he told his assistant, Dervin, after a last look at his communications screen. "Mercs en route to 38th quadrant, stopping here to discharge passengers." He tapped his desktop thoughtfully. "Two passengers."

"On a Merc ship? That's weird. And only two?"

"From Thelona."

"Where the hell is Thelona?"

"45th quadrant," Roger replied. "Fairly

backwards place. One Thelonian, one Danaali—a really backwards place."

Dervin appeared to busy himself stirring café the dispenser never dispensed quite to his satisfaction, but he was taking it all in. "Sounds like we'll have our work cut out for us."

"Oh, I don't know. We've had worse. Remember when the Dinovians tried to burn the place down?"

"Vividly."

"Well, these two have requested asylum and the Mercs don't give just anybody a ride. So I suspect one or both of them has run afoul of something political on Thelona."

"What's political on Thelona?"

"I have no idea."

"Want me to go meet them? You know, just in case they're the burning type."

"Not likely," Roger speculated. "One is a

woman. But sure. I've got that hydroponics thing to go to. They're due in at 13:00 hours, bay 3. Could be interesting. Buzz me up if there's a problem."

"Will do."

* * * *

Lela's first impression of Twelve was positive if only because it lacked the blazing suns that had nearly immolated her when she disembarked at Thelona. There appeared to be only one sun and it was not intense—rather, it seemed to slant a muted welcome across a small city punctuated by squares of startling silver grass. She held to Caius as he bid an appropriately grateful farewell to the mercenaries who had smuggled them off Thelona in the face of Imperial wrath. They had not quite risked their lives, as even the Highest would not challenge a ship full of Mercs, but she and Caius had certainly risked theirs.

"Yes, fare well," she added to the captain who had taken them unerringly across galaxies and time. It was amazing to her that these people did it on a regular basis, abandoning homes and families for a life in the stars.

"And you," he replied graciously. "Be well and happy."

There were no troops awaiting them, no guards, no one but a smallish red-haired man who smiled disarmingly.

"Welcome, travelers. I am Dervin, the assistant to our Governor. He could not be here, but sends his greeting."

"It is appreciated," Caius said. "I am Caius, Scion of the House of Bardin on

Thelona. This is my companion, Lela."

"Interesting name," Dervin noted. "Caius. Sounds similar to one from our ancient Earth history."

"As I believe it was given," Caius agreed. "My father was well versed in Earth literature. He admired your ancient Romans. They are famous everywhere, you know. I do not think it's a coincidence I have the name."

"Lovely coincidence," Dervin said, gesturing to a shaded portico away from the landing pad where their transport sat, circled by busy attendants preparing it to return to space. It would not linger, Caius had told her. The Mercs were needed elsewhere, further on, fighting their mercenary battles at the behest of the air companies. Some of those they had flown with would be dead a month hence. "What brings you to us?"

"Trouble on my planet," Caius said candidly. "There was insurrection, I sought to assist the survivors and it was taken ill by our Highest who had not the best opinion of me to begin with. It seemed advisable to leave and you were recommended by friends in the Mercenary Corps."

"Merc, were you?"

Caius nodded. "Eight years in the Corps. I do not mind relocating elsewhere. For Lela," he acknowledged her, "it may be otherwise. But she could not remain."

"Understood. Well, come inside and take refreshment if you will. I will need to do some documentation for you."

"I have brought what you will need," Caius said.

"Of course." Dervin smiled at her and Lela thought it was genuine. This man had been sent in part because of his charm, but she could sense no guile in him. She also thought he was not a fool.

The building they entered was like none she had seen—an edifice of hard material like the ship, generously studded with glass. She could see people going down corridors where moving hallways offered various directions. Caius was right; it was much like the ship. As they landed, she had seen several such buildings, all linked by walkways made of some shining substance. It was a smaller city than the Thelonian capitol of Syrstine, but it had the advantage of not being on fire.

"We'll meet in my office and then get you some housing, all right?" Dervin inquired, moving them without delay through hallways filled with people, plants reaching to the sun through many windows and a pleasant background of modulated music—nondescript but soothing. There was what appeared to be a central fountain and, beyond that, he took them through a doorway where a woman scarcely older than Lela greeted them pleasantly. Like the rest, she wore a smartly tailored gray suit of trousers and tunic. Lela found it interesting, and significant. On Thelona, even on her native Danaali, you could tell at once by someone's dress essentially where they came from and what they did. Not so on Twelve. All dressed alike, just as they all appeared to use Standard Speech. For herself, she had draped a coverlet strategically over the sheer-bodiced gown that announced she was exactly what she appeared—a woman who slept with men.

The young woman who assisted Dervin brought café. Lela was familiar with it from the ship and observed Caius's caution that she should take only liquids at first. "Are you able to partake of food yet?" Dervin inquired, so that she knew he understood their travel, and Caius shook his head.

"Tomorrow, perhaps."

"Yes, I understand. Well, you will need some rest shortly, but first may I review your papers?"

It was not a request, but they knew that. Caius handed over documents without protest and then he and Lela sipped while their new host satisfied himself as to their credentials. Caius had a legal mind and, even running for his life, had not forgotten to bring those.

"These appear to be in good order," Dervin finally said. "You have some administrative skill, I see." This he directed to Caius.

"The law-speaker degree is fairly

universal, I believe," Caius replied smoothly, "although, of course, I will take pains to acquaint myself with your laws, if I may. Perhaps I may then be of some assistance to you."

"A man with both legal and mercenary experience?" Dervin chuckled. "Oh, yes, I think you can help. We do not have an influx of settlers at present, but they always come and we need someone who can sort them out and handle troublemakers if they have slipped in. And I think..." he gave Caius a level look, "you can handle troublemakers."

"Assuredly."

"So I thought." Derval affixed a seal to his documents, apparently admitting him to the Colony. "And you..." He turned to Lela. "What would be your preference?"

Well, that was getting right down to it,

she thought. If you came to Twelve, you worked. She thought it unnecessary to reveal that her occupation was whoring. It had not been by choice, after all.

"I am good with child care," she said slowly. "And plants. I have seen you have them. And animals?"

"An agricultural worker, then, I think," Dervin defined her. "We do not eat animals by choice, but we have a very fine collection of endangered species from Earth, perpetuated here for their pleasure and ours. Do you think you would like to tend them?"

"Oh, yes!"

"Very good." Their host sealed her papers. "Just sign here if you will or…"

"I will sign for both," Caius said. She had begun to learn that once, Lela thought ruefully, but that had not lasted. Still, in the face of everything intimidating and new, she found it a nice touch that their entrance to the planet was enabled by the time-honored tradition of a written signature. Not all the graces had been lost.

"We will give you rooms to begin," Dervin said. "I assume you wish to be together?"

"Quite." Again Caius spoke for her and Lela saw the other man glance at her fleetingly, as if wondering about it. But when she didn't speak, he handed Caius a card.

"Here is a pass you may use to move from one place to another. Anything off limits is clearly marked. This will purchase food and clothing for you. We all share equally here. Simply take what you need and no more. Many of us dine communally, we enjoy it, but that choice is your own. There are food courts when you are ready where you may eat or take food out. There are directions on each wall, in Standard Speech and also marked."

He smiled at Lela. "Not everyone reads it. Take a day or two to rest, enjoy our gardens, and then we will begin your residence. There is an excellent library, also." Lela knew this was said for Caius's benefit. "Our days are 36 hours, it may take you some little time to adjust, but you will. There is but one sun, one moon, and the nights are dark. There are torches in your room if you should wish to go outside after dark. You are safe enough within the city, though there is a guard. You may ask them for any help required. Any questions?"

Caius looked at Lela, but she shook her head.

"In half a year's time, if you wish to remain, you may apply for citizenship."

"That is very generous," Caius acknowledged the courtesy. "We are grateful."

"You may not be, when you see how much there is to learn." Dervin laughed. "But most people do stay. The folk here are friendly. I think you will be the only Thelonian, and they may be curious."

"That was often the case when I was in the Corps," Caius surprised Lela by admitting. She was accustomed to a man some inches taller than most humans, whose eyes could turn blood red with temper on occasion. But she supposed others could be put off. "I am used to it."

"Then my assistant will show you to your quarters. They will do for the time being though they will not be permanent. And be welcome."

Easy…it was so easy, Lela thought as

they followed the brisk young assistant to the rooms. She had gone through far more arriving on Thelona as a slave. She did not like to think of what had been required of her upon her arrival. She could sense nothing of that savage compulsion or inhumanity on this planet…only good order and peace.

She hoped it was not too good to last. She also hoped Caius could stand it.

Chapter Three

"That girl is a slave," Dervin said.

Roger merely looked at him with brows lifted.

"She did a good job concealing it," Dervin admitted, "but she's wearing slave dress. I saw it on Regus 8. He's dangerous, probably a revolutionary, and got himself in trouble. Then he took off with a slave girl he fancied."

"She all right?"

"I think so. The medico sent medical records with her, so I suspect she wondered about it, too. But the girl acts like she's afraid to let him out of her sight, so she's either intimidated or attached to him."

"Yes, I read those," Roger said. "Any redeeming qualities?"

Dervin scratched his incipient red beard. He had never had it eliminated and periodically—usually when he wakened late and didn't shave—it threatened to return. "No weapons. Nothing suspect."

"So what are we going to do with them?"

"I've got them in housing for now. She brightened up considerably when I told her we had an animal sanctuary. She can work up there. If he can control himself, he'd make a good Guard. He brought along a law-speaking degree I doubted, but it is legitimate. Turns out Thelona isn't that backwards. He's Guild-registered. Very intelligent. Well spoken. He knows his way around."

"We might have another job for him,

then," Roger observed. "There's an old expression for a guy like that…hanging judge. I could use one."

Dervin guffawed. "I checked his financials, too. Got credits all over the galaxy."

"How long did you say he was in the Mercs?"

"Eight years."

"Time enough to make a fortune, depending on who he killed. Well, have the Guard keep an eye on him. He'll beat them or join them, I expect."

"He's not like anything we've got."

Roger shrugged. "He's a Merc. Sometimes they can readjust to civilian life, sometimes not. But when you've got something like Dinovians landing, they can be damn handy. Let's give it a little time."

Roger remained, fingers tented, studying

his viewscreen at some length after Dervin had gone back to his own office. The Governor had learned to trust his assistant's judgment. Dervin might be somewhat quick to judge the weak spots in any immigration request, but he had been proven right more than once. Roger did not always make a habit of reviewing such requests so carefully, leaving those matters largely to his assistant. But he was studying the medical records of a woman who had no idea he had them. He doubted she even knew what they were or that they had been obtained while she lay in stasis. That was simply standard procedure, but in this instance, they had been of note.

Her Lord was, in all probability, a firebrand. But that did not so much concern Roger. There were as yet no political divisions to be exploited in his tiny domain. If that Merc energy could be channeled in a positive direction, Caius of the House of Bardin could prove to be an asset.

If, on the other hand, he had inflicted the damages Roger was seeing…well, that was another matter. No woman would be treated that way while he was Governor. As precept of a still-small colony, he had eyes and ears everywhere.

This pair bore watching.

Chapter Four

It might have been worth sleeping twelve years.

Even the sun here agreed with her, Lela thought, stretching luxuriously in the last rays of the day. Above her on one of the gentle hills, she could see the tiny figures of goats—Earth creatures similar to nonnis—grazing eagerly on the silvery grass that had so surprised her. Silver or not, it was nutritious and they relished it. She, in turn, loved to make them happy. They were like the innocent creatures from her youth, even more pleasing because here on Twelve, no one ate them.

Caius, freed from a day of study, was

walking from the goat pen to her perch on a rock used as a lookout spot. There were few wild animals on Twelve and they seemed to avoid the settlement, where they had learned to fear powered fences that stung. Still, Lela was a careful shepherd and this day she had help. Smiling, she reached for his hand, which he took to pull her up and against him.

"You smell like goat," she said happily.

"As well I should." For once, Caius did not wear the ubiquitous gray uniform Lela found comfortable but monotonous. Instead, he had changed back into his own clothing for the task of fence-fixing—not the long-distance fences that were magnetized, but the ones penning livestock near the barn. Those were old-fashioned wood, not shocking to the animals, which were sometimes pregnant ewes.

But they were also chewable and he had donated his free day to their repair.

Lela leaned deliberately against him, more in comfort than invitation. That would come later, in their own bed, in their own house—modest though it might be.

"This reminds me of Cas Solar," she said.

"Yes," Caius agreed quietly, so quietly that she thought perhaps it was unwise to remind him of his beloved summer home. "And you are still the nonni-girl."

"I am." She looked up at him questioningly. "Are you not happy here?"

"Passably."

Oh, no, it was as she had feared. They were aging now, out of stasis. What of their friends left behind on Thelona? Did they live? Did they have children? Children of children? The one thing she could not have. She had

Caius, and her freedom. It was more than she had ever envisioned. She should be grateful, and she was. But she thought it was not enough for him.

"Time to bring these animals in?" he asked.

"If the fence is fixed, yes. Otherwise I'll be chasing them from here to Capitol." It was no idle threat. Plants from Earth, transported at great cost to the Colony, were precious and the goats preferred them to any other provender. They would elude her with great determination in order to stuff those into their four-chambered stomachs, which could hold a dismaying amount. It would take hours to retrieve them.

"It's fixed."

* * * *

Home was a simple block-shaped residence on the outskirts of the small workers' village near the animal compound. There were few private vehicles on Twelve. Most people walked to their employment and recreation, so proximity to the job was a good thing and their little house had simply been given to them. As they had been told, people lived collectively, with all expenses and all proceeds distributed to the whole. Since no one lacked anything, few were greedy. If they were, Caius dealt with them in court. Roger had been acting as their law-giver, but he had multitudes of responsibilities and was more than happy to give Caius that job as soon as he had completed requisite studies.

Lela had hoped it would be enough for him, but it was becoming increasingly obvious that it wasn't.

"Are you sure you want to eat here?" she asked, entering their unlocked dwelling.

"Why? Didn't you make anything?"

"Of course I did." Lela's long-abandoned talent for cooking from a limited supply had come in handy. She had not always eaten meat as a child because meat was for sale, not consumption by the farmer who raised it. It was too valuable. So she had long since learned to cook with grains and vegetables, both of which were readily available on Twelve, where they eschewed meat not because they were poor but because they were compassionate.

"I just hoped you might like to eat at the Hall, that's all."

Caius shook his head, dashing her hope.

"Why do you hold yourself apart from the people? Are you afraid that you will have to judge them someday?"

"Partly. But I don't particularly care to be an attraction."

Lela sighed. He was not mistaken. People did stare at them just a bit. Most denizens were human. There were no other Thelonians and no couples of different races who were bonded. A few women had commented to her that Caius was very handsome, but what she thought they meant was that he was handsome *in his way*. Nor did she think they quite accepted her, though she was careful to keep her revealing gowns for private moments. Still, she supposed people were the same on every planet. They liked to talk.

Dervin and Roger, who had introduced himself to them simply as Roger, were different. Despite or perhaps because of their elevated positions, they were approachable and outgoing. Still, she and Caius were left largely to their own devices and that also was beginning to not be enough.

What they needed, she acknowledged to herself, was a child. It would have opened a door into the community they could not enter without one. Children were highly valued on Twelve, they represented its future and, feeling safe at last, she had abandoned the hair decorations her mother had filled with ladiesbane to help her abort any children conceived in slavery. But just as Idamastine the midwife on Thelona had warned her, losing three such children had damaged her. She was barren.

Silently she dished up root stew she had made that morning, with bread and goat cheese. But at least Caius ate with good appetite. She thought the manual labor at the sanctuary suited him, burning up energy he might otherwise have expended in less productive ways. One thing the residents did have in common with other planets was liquor, and she knew its effects on Caius. But, thus far at least, he had not touched it. Perhaps he feared the same thing she did. They had no cold pool any more where he could clear his aching head nor Gracchu, his large house guard who had been able to handle him. Temperance was no longer just a virtue, but a necessity.

The sun was fully set by the time they finished and she touched the glow-lamps for light, still momentarily startled each time they leapt into life at her touch. This was when Caius would retreat into his readings, still learning the differences in law on Twelve, while she amused herself by…well, mostly remembering. From a comfortable chair, granted. But the memories were not comforting.

"What do you want to do, Caius?" she finally asked when the silence had gone on too long.

"Do?" Clearly surprised, he put down the touch screen he had been using. "What do you mean?"

"Do," she repeated, with an assurance that was new to her. But she was a free woman now. "You are not happy here. You are bored and restless. I can feel it."

He made a dismissive gesture. "It's of no importance. I have work, we have a means to live, it is what everyone has here. We have safety. No rulers, no burning cities, no pestilence or people rioting in the streets."

"And no going back."

"You want to go back?"

"Not I," she protested, "but I think you do."

"Another twelve years in stasis? Oh, I don't think so. And as far as I know the Highest is still in power. We'd be killed the moment we got there. There was no means to effectuate any change there, Lela. Here we have some influence on the future."

"Do we?"

"What do you mean?'

"Children, Caius. We have none, nor can we ever. What future is that?"

Abruptly, he stood, walked over, knelt at her chair. Never had he done such a thing.

"So that is what is bothering you." She realized then that he had been as much aware of her trouble as she had been of his. He just had never spoken of it. "Lela, I told you before and I tell you again, it does not matter to me. If that is your fear, put it away. If it is *your* fear, speak to someone. I am sure there is a way to have some child if it is a child you need— maybe not ours, but another. Talk to Roger. He knows everything that goes on in this colony."

"I did," she confessed. "He knows of no orphans. Caius, people here don't die. No one is old enough yet and they have healing chambers. Very, very seldom do they lose anyone. All the children have homes—good homes. They have no need of us."

"Well, ask him again. You never know what can happen."

As if determined to fulfill his words, his communicator buzzed. He looked startled, almost affronted. Their first serious conversation, Lela thought in exasperation, and someone called. No one ever called. Why now?

Perhaps it was good they had. Watching

Caius's expression change, she grew certain of it. He spoke quietly, but there was animation in his face she had not seen in…almost forever. He clicked off, standing.

"There is some trouble at the landing site, Roger is asking me to come in."

There was never anything more than a dust storm on Twelve. "What kind?"

"They have a freighter with crew that has given them trouble before."

"But you're not a Guard!" Lela protested. "Why you?"

"Why not me?" In two strides, he reached the door and beside it, where he had kept a scatter pistol since they arrived. It was mainly intended for anything that threatened the animals, but of course there were other uses as well.

"He's sending a transport." This was

notable. "You should stay here. There is another gun in there if you need it."

"Of all the flaming," she muttered. "Who are these troublemakers?"

"Dinovians."

If she hadn't been sitting, her knees would have buckled. Of all the horrors that could ever have pursued her...Dinovians. Twelve was supposedly light years away from the race she had first seen in Thelona's quadrant. She knew they were far-flung ore miners and traders, but here? If they, too, had found Twelve—how safe was it?

"Oh, Caius. They are lethal."

He looked at her piercingly. "You know of them?

"Yes."

He strapped on his pistol. "Stay here, Lela, I mean it. There is another scatter gun in here," and he gestured to the storage unit. "Don't hesitate to use it."

"I won't," she said grimly. Privately, she wondered if she would simply freeze up in fear at the sight of one of those monsters. On the other hand, she had a score to settle with them.

There was the whirling noise of a transport outside and through the glass she could see their external glow lights kick on, illuminating a dust cloud from the descending craft. She could also see the figures of other men running from their houses, towards it. Roger must have roused the village in addition to the Guards and her heart sank.

"Stay safe!" was all she had time to tell Caius, and then he was gone, on the run, out and into the transport almost faster than she could think. When she could....when its noise was fading into the distance...she locked their door for the first time.

Dinovians. She still could not believe they were on Twelve. Roger would never have given them landing rights if they had been trouble in the past, so that meant this was unscheduled and probably punitive. They were notoriously vindictive, Dinovians. She remembered them—their color, dark, but not like other humanoid races who merely had darker skins. Dark and nearly alien, though they could and did interbreed with humans. She knew that only too well. She vividly recalled their smell—metallic and revolting…and their size. Dearly as she honored him, Caius and his scatter pistol were no match for an enraged Dinovian with weapons.

She still bore the scars of their beatings, not where anyone could see them but inside. Deep inside, body and soul. Scars so profound she had not wanted to live, not cared, had stopped fighting to survive, only wanting it to be over until Caius had found her in the slave market and given her a reason to exist. She could not lose him or she would lose herself, this time forever.

Chapter Five

Roger had never expected Twelve to be invaded, still, he had prepared for it. Caius whistled as their Governor and Dervin opened the door to a weapons depot he had never suspected they had.

The two administrators dove inside like Earth beavers Caius had seen at wooded lands above the sanctuary, handing out weapons with a few words and great speed.

"Tacticals," Roger said, tossing one to Caius. He caught it with ease, familiar with the laser-focused weapons and their lighted scopes. Those would cast a beam when they locked on target and were intended for night fighting or nocturnal predators. The men should already know how to use them.

"Grenades. Press the button to detonate. You only have a few seconds, so don't blow yourselves up."

This remark he addressed not to Caius, who knew it, but to the assembled crowd of men outside the door. None of these were Guards. They were farmers and men from the small start-up mine outside the city limits—men accustomed to dangerous equipment and heavy physical work. In the absence of Earth troops who were too far away to be of immediate help, they would have to do.

"Caius, you know the use of these, and deployment." Caius nodded. "Dervin and I will take half the men, you take the other. Guards have the Dinovians ringed in the southeast quarter, but without more fire power, they will break through."

He spoke to the men. "They are miners and we expect they will make for the mines, to try to establish control of them and stand us off. They will go through your families on the way and I don't have to tell you what will happen. We threw them off planet last time, this time we have to kill them or more will come." Roger paused for a moment, accepting the inevitable. "More may come anyway."

Yes, Caius thought. If more aggressive species had discovered their idyllic planet with its newly-tapped resources, Earth could not wholly defend them. They would have to do it themselves.

"Caius, we will have need of you. I am putting you in charge because you have Mercenary experience." Caius sensed a stir among the men, some of whom had not known it. "We will need you afterwards, too, so try not to get killed."

There was a ripple of nervous laughter.

"They have armor and you do not," Roger counseled the group, "so use everything possible for cover. Your tacticals are armor-piercing, but don't shoot till you've got a target. Their power supply won't last indefinitely. If it extinguishes, that's when you use grenades—or if you see a group, don't try to shoot individually. Just blow the bastards up."

"It is more likely to be hand to hand," Caius advised. "If the citizens lock down, they will go into the buildings after them. So be careful who you blow up."

"Right," Roger agreed. "Let's go."

Everyone knew the southeast quarter. The group split almost without instruction in a flanking maneuver, running as silently as possible through streets where glow lights no longer functioned. There were no lights in the buildings, either, and Caius suspected Roger had cut power to give his citizens cover and increase the element of surprise. Their affable leader was revealing a side of himself Caius had not expected. He had thought Roger was a bureaucrat. Then again, most of the men had not known that he, himself, had been a hired killer.

With a rush of pure adrenaline-fueled battle fever that was almost joy, he accepted that he still was.

* * * *

He slowed the men, practicing caution, when they reached the quarter. Nobody had an accurate count of the enemy, who could be anywhere, and their dark color would help to further disguise them. He was sure they would have worn non-reflective body armor. His Thelonian eyes enabled him to see somewhat more acutely than the humans could, but even he would have difficulty making them out. The one thing they couldn't disguise was their smell. Dinovians, to him, smelled like something burning and he would be happy to make that a reality.

"Smell for them," he told the men in a whisper. "Like old, wet charcoal." The miners knew that scent. Fanning out, they crept through the night. The moon was shrouded, waning and clouded. The sons of mothers had timed this carefully, Caius thought.

Abruptly, he knew where they were. Motioning quickly to the others, he wended his way like a scenting hound toward the main administrative building. There would be no staff working at night, but it housed them and their families. The Dinovians were going for their weak underbelly—unarmed civilians. It wasn't the ultimate goal—control of the mines was—but they would wreak havoc on their way, cutting off communications and exulting in carnage.

It was so silent inside that he knew the residents had locked down, but that wouldn't be much protection. The Dinovians would explode their doors.

Punctuating the silence, he heard such a resounding boom. It gave him and the other men a location and they responded instantly, sprinting down one of the unmoving hallways whose treads were turned off. In a moment, they were guided by screams.

A barely-seen form loomed up in the dark. Cauis aimed his tactical, unerringly, and the scope sprang to life. Pinned in its glare, a fully armed Dinovian attempted to respond, but he was already dead. Caius's laser had sliced through his neck.

Chaos erupted. The weapons fire was silent, but the Dinovians were not. Cursing and raving, they curtailed their murder of Twelve's citizens to turn on its avenging fighters.

"Guard the hall!" Caius roared to some of the men, engaging whatever had invaded the residential apartments. "They'll be coming." Locked in the finely-taught precision reflex drummed into him by Mercenary masters, he took a couple of Dinovians before they could respond. They had expected nothing more than screaming women and children, but what they got was Thelonian hell.

True to his prediction, behind him Caius heard his miners and farmers firing. Dinovians acted like a swarm, flocking to the defense of besieged comrades, but it made them vulnerable. Faced with a frontal charge, Caius's men simply fired until their weapons were hot.

He was astonished by their courage. Two men were down, probably dead, but a small horde of Dinovians lay sprawled in a bloody mess across the hallway, in both directions. Inside the apartment, someone was crying, but he had no time to investigate.

"Stay down!" he yelled inside the doorway. The door was shattered and the inhabitants would have no cover; they would simply have to hide wherever they could. He had more work to do.

They cleared the building, faced with stiff

resistance once the Dinovians knew they were there, but apparently the colonists outnumbered them. Driven by the fear that their families would be murdered, the colonists fought like maniacs. Defenders nearly always had the psychological advantage, Caius knew. They had more to lose. There was no question that his men would fight.

Fight they did, through the building and onto the street and then another building and then another street, up and down in a pattern he directed. Caius and his men blew up the streets without compunction whenever they could get more than a single shooter on them, and screams and explosions from the other side of the quarter informed him others were doing the same. The offices made good shelter, either permitting them to duck around corners or sprint between buildings under covering fire.

Men were hit, but his were smaller and faster than the Dinovians.

He had faced far worse. These were actually manageable numbers, he thought coolly, and perhaps manageable casualties as well. Eventually he began to see guards in their distinctive uniforms, filtering back in from the perimeter they had established. Assisted by the men from the villages, they had been able to hold it and retreat inward, pinning Dinovians between two forces, killing as they went. Their forces met in the street, panting and exhausted.

The guards had torches and swept large circles around them. Everything was clear but for the dead and street rubble.

"Brother," the chief guard greeted Caius. They were briefly acquainted from Caius's time judging some recalcitrants the chief had brought to his bench, but he had never expected such a greeting. It was the bond of war, race and position forgotten.

"Are you whole?" Caius inquired.

"No, we have dead." Laser fire was usually mortal. "They have more."

"Thanks be for that, at least," Caius muttered. Adrenaline spent, he was feeling the ravages of battle—nothing physical, as he was unharmed. But he knew well the sadness of loss, although these were not his people.

Or were they? He had killed for them; he had defended their lives. He supposed they were as much his as anyone's, now. But it was time for cleanup. He would see if their fondness lasted beyond the consecration of their dead.

Chapter Six

Lela virtually dove for her communicator when it buzzed. Like most technology, it intimidated her and she used it only reluctantly—but not that day. It had to be Caius. Please, let it be him and not someone to tell her he was dead.

It was Caius.

"I'm all right," he said at once. "Not hurt. Are you all right there?"

"Perfect," she assured him. They had seen explosions from Capitol that had scared them badly, but the village had remained untouched.

"We prevailed," he said, "but we have

dead and there is damage. I will have to stay here for a while. I just wanted to see if you were safe."

"Very safe," she said, faintly.

"Good. Please stay, then. There is nothing you can do here that we cannot and you have the animals to care for. I will come as soon as I can."

"Were there many?"

"Not too many. Don't worry about me, Lela. I have been through much worse."

She was sure he had, but she hadn't. She couldn't let him know.

"You're right, I should care for the animals. They were upset by the explosions."

"The power is out here. Some of the streets are wrecked and we've got a lot of dead Dinovians to get rid of."

"Colonists?"

"Some of those, too."

"Oh, Caius…"

"I know. I'll call if it's anyone we know."

If it was anyone they knew. Well, they didn't actually know that many people. Perhaps she should be glad. In the meantime, she told herself, she should do her job. Just do the work. It would steady her.

It did, to an extent. When the animals were fed, she ate a solitary, uneasy dinner while the sun fell. She had just finished when there was a chime at the still-locked door. For the first time, she took the precaution of checking the view screen before answering and sucked in her breath in shock at what—at who—she saw.

It was Roger. Roger, Governor of their Colony, at her door. Not the immaculate, articulate Roger she had always seen and he was not alone. She buzzed the door open at once.

"What is it?" she blurted. This Roger was disheveled, red-eyed, sweat- and soot-stained and cradling a toddler baby against his chest.

"May I come in?"

"Of course, of course." Flustered, she fell back to admit him, then instinctively reached to touch the sleeping infant. "What…"

Roger smiled, a twisted smile that looked suspiciously close to weeping.

"You wanted a baby, I believe?"

She just nodded. Oh, this could not be the way her prayers would be answered…or could it?

"Well, I have one for you." Unasked, he sank into a chair, carefully so as not to wake the child. Her thumb was in her mouth and her chubby little legs straddled his hips, but she never stirred. She looked dirty and exhausted, with tear tracks down her face. "I know I told you we had no orphans, but…" his voice broke, "we do now."

"I am so sorry," she said softly. This man was about to go over the edge. One push, one wrong word, and he was going to go. Then he would never be able to forget that she had seen his weakness.

"This is my niece," he said.

"Oh…no," she breathed.

"My sister and her husband lived in the administrative center. The Dinovians came there first, to cut off our communications. After they had, they went to the apartments. Blew off the doors, killed everyone they could find. It was dark and they missed the baby in her cot."

"Dearest gods." It seemed to be all she could say. But she wondered why her uncle was not taking the baby home with him.

"I have no one to care for her." His voice broke again. "My wife is dead."

This time Lela couldn't restrain herself. The moan that came out was wrenched from her soul. While this good man had been saving their colony, enemies had killed his entire family. This tiny child was all that was left. If she had hated Dinovians before, now she loathed them with an acrid, boiling fury.

"She needs goat's milk," he said tonelessly, as if this explained his choice of caretaker. "She cannot tolerate cow's and the artificial milk did not suit her."

"Oh, of course, naturally," Lela stuttered. "We have plenty here. Yes, of course I will keep her, for as long as you need. What is her name?"

"Anuska. She is eighteen months."

He looked like he would fall over. His fine blond hair was streaked with blood and she didn't know if it was his and didn't want to ask. It was not dripping, so he wasn't badly hurt.

"Well, you just give Anuska here to me," she said, with far more confidence than she felt. Oh, she could not let him come apart. He couldn't. They needed him. Yet how could anyone bear such a loss? "I am so terribly sorry, Roger."

"I know. Just keep her for me, please."

"Anything," she promised, taking the soundly sleeping child from his arms. In the back of her mind she already knew she would love this child and then Roger would patch his life together and take her back, and then her heart would break. But it was nothing compared to his devastation.

"She will be safe here with us." No one would be safe if the Dinovians came back and she knew it, but Lela offered what comfort she could. She knew Caius would not object. He had never actually confessed to any desire for children, she realized. He had not even said whether he liked them. The point had been moot since she couldn't have any. But she couldn't conceive of him denying Roger's request.

Somehow Anuska's uncle dragged himself to his feet again, heading for the door.

"Do you want me to ask for a transport?" she called behind him, but he shook his head.

"I'd rather walk."

"But it's dark!"

"I have a torch. Just let me walk, Lela."

She too had known grief that made you want to walk sightlessly into the void, so she didn't try to stop him.

"My gods be with you," she said softly to his departing figure, "since you have none of your own."

Chapter Seven

Boldly as she might have spoken to Roger, she had no means to care for a baby, so as soon as he had gone she lit her own torch and carried Anuska to the communal Hall where she might find what she needed. It was locked and silent, reflecting a new reality in all their lives, and she had to buzz for admission.

She was only slightly acquainted with the woman who answered, but a baby was a universal passcode.

"I've been brought an orphan to care for," she said without further explanation. No doubt word would get out soon enough, but Roger deserved what moments of privacy she could give him. "I need things for her."

"Oh, the poor baby!" As she had expected, help and pity were immediately forthcoming. "Bring her in, bring her in."

Then, at last, the baby roused, whimpering and clinging to a warm body, even if it was one she didn't know. Lela rocked her slowly, rubbing her back, afraid of wails. But Anuska continued only to cry in deep, choking whimpers that hurt her heart more badly than if she had screamed. She sounded broken.

"Oh, poor, poor thing," the matron, Simla, repeated, but Lela couldn't tell which of them she was addressing. At that moment, she felt nearly as bereft as the baby, momentarily questioning Roger's wisdom in leaving her with a woman he barely knew. But she was that woman, she told herself. She had a duty.

She was fortunate with Simla, who

ransacked through the Hall where everyone brought their children to eat. Most brought their own supplies, but you never knew, and things were on hand. Quickly, she assembled a carryall of soft cups and feeding bottles, nappies, a couple of clean gowns kept for children who soiled theirs…whatever Lela might need.

"She can have only goat's milk," Lela told her, smoothing the baby's little tufts of hair, blond like her uncle's. No one could mistake this for any but a human child, she thought with a pang. Nothing like what she and Caius would have had. Her own child, she knew, would have looked Thelonian. The crosses always did. But no use to think of that. She had a baby, at least for a time. She watched as Simla assembled containers of the precious goat's milk and stuffed them into the carryall.

"You have food for her?" she asked, and Lela nodded. "You know what to feed her?"

Lela smiled. Yes, no doubt the women had talked. They knew or suspected that she was just a pretty bedmate, probably a slave in her past, without much life experience as they knew it. They might not trust her in this endeavor. But she trusted herself.

"I know what to feed her."

"Come, I'll walk you back with a torch," Simla offered. "You've got your hands full."

She did, so Lela accepted the help. What she also got was a running discourse all the short distance back to her home as she alternately bounced the baby and tried to satisfy the other woman's curiosity.

"Pretty bad, I think," she answered the immediate spate of questions about the fate of their capitol. "Caius said there were dead and he must stay to help, then someone brought me this baby. Her parents were killed. I'm just to keep her for a time." Even to herself, she could not think this baby would stay with them. It was only a temporary arrangement. She could not get too attached.

On the other hand, how not to pour out love and compassion on this little one, so cruelly wrenched from her life on an idyllic, gentle planet where she had only been sheltered and adored? Suddenly, Lela thought, their lives were as hard as everyone else's. She had been living a dream. No planet she'd ever been on was peaceful. There was war and rumors of war—where had she heard that? But it was true. People fighting for scraps. People dying for rocks in the ground or waters on the earth. Always death.

Finally, the baby was truly crying, as if

she had come to the same realization that life was dangerous, so she took a hasty leave of Simla. There was no bed for the child, but she and Caius had plenty of room in theirs, and then she laughed to herself. How would a sadly reduced Lord of Rank deal with living like everyone else—tiny house, smelly nappies and a squirming infant on his pillow? She had never envisioned Caius that way. She was sure he had never pictured it, either.

* * * *

He called again shortly after she had finally gotten Anuska to sleep in their bed, carefully propped with pillows. The baby was fed, clean, changed and safe. She was exhausted.

"Are you well?" was all he asked.

"Fine. What is happening?"

"Cleanup," he replied succinctly.

"Have you seen Roger?" If he had, he might know of her present situation.

"Roger? No. He's extremely busy."

Not too busy to walk to my house, Lela thought, but she knew why he had done it. The destruction in his city he could handle, the loss of life he could not. Walking away from it, if only to place his niece, had probably saved his sanity.

"He was here."

"There? At the village?"

"Here at our house," she clarified. "He brought me a little girl to care for."

There was a long silence at the other end.

"Caius, it's his niece." She heard the tears in her own voice. "Her parents were killed. And Roger's wife—she's gone, too."

"Oh my gods! We had not heard. He's locked up in his office, working."

First, he had sought safety for his family. This time. He had not done it when all the Colonists' lives had depended on him and she knew he would never forgive himself. She had not spoken with him overly much, no more than any other Colonist with a problem. But even from that brief contact, she knew he was a man of deep conscience.

"I told him I would keep her as long as he needed. Is it all right?"

"Yes," he said at once and she relaxed a fist she had not known she had clenched as they spoke.

"I will be back tomorrow," he promised. "I will try to find him to tell him so. Of course she can stay. Do you need anything for her?"

"I have it all. She is just little."

"All right." He seemed to hesitate. "Take care of both of you."

"I will."

She clicked off. He was busy. But she knew she needed to sleep. There were animals to feed in the morning and she would have to find a way to carry the baby with her. Her life would have to change and she was going to be busy, too.

Peacetime was over.

Chapter Eight

He came home when he said he would, but he was not the same.

He still wore the clothes he had worn to repair the goat pen, stained and dirty now, but they were Thelonian clothes. He looked once more like a Thelonian Lord and not only because he wore them. There was a fierceness in his face she had not seen since they had left his home and she studied him surreptitiously.

He was humanoid but not fully human, a fact she had not quite appreciated until she was back among her own kind. Thelonians had caramel colored skin because otherwise their two strong suns would have cooked them to a cinder. Every one she had ever seen had his deep-set amber eyes and mane of reddish-brown hair, but Caius also had a broad brow, a nose that would have been aquiline except that it had been broken, and a sensual mouth. His body she knew intimately—virtually perfect and a deep source of pleasure to her. His strength was prodigious.

He looked akin to one of the wild gods of her people's myths. He loved her like one, too, deeply carnal and demanding. She wanted him, badly and right then, but had a child clinging to her tunic.

"Hello, little girl," he said gently, but he did not approach. The child was staring at him with saucer-like eyes. It was time to make the introduction, Lela thought—slowly and carefully. She opened her mouth to begin and was cut off mid-breath by the first words she had heard out of Anuska.

"Bad man!"

The child could speak, and quite well, in perfect Standard Speech. There could be no doubt what she had said.

"Oh, no, Anuska," she said quickly. "This is not a bad man. This is Caius. He is *my* man."

She saw something fleeting yet profound in Caius's expression, then it was gone.

"She remembers," he said. "She saw what happened. To her, I look like one of the bad men. She's afraid."

"You look nothing like a Dinovian." But Lela squatted quickly to take the stiff little girl in her arms. "He is my friend, Anuska. He is not like the bad men."

The child whimpered, not convinced, thrusting her thumb deep into her mouth.

"Hush, baby," Lela whispered,

unnecessarily. Anuska couldn't possibly speak past the impediment of her thumb. "It's all right, little love."

"It's going to take more than that," Caius observed, turning to open their storage compartment. Sliding his scatter gun inside, he hit the security button on the door as it closed. It would open only to his finger pad or Lela's, not to the child's. It had never been locked before.

He turned back to observe the little girl, somberly. "It's going to take time." But then, like a flash of light in a dark place, he gifted Lela with one of his genuine and rare full smiles. "Just like with you."

She flushed, but it was true. It had taken moons for him to entice her to share his bed, longer still to gain her trust. In some ways, she realized, he was still doing it. This would be one of those times.

"Get her something she really likes to eat," he suggested. "Give her a good memory instead of what she has."

"You, too," Lela commented, lifting the unresisting baby onto her hip. "Come and eat. I'm sure you haven't."

"Not much," he agreed.

"I have no chair for her," she complained, opening the cold box.

"Put her in the sink."

It was a brilliant idea. Lela cocked her head at him, frankly amazed. "How did you know that?"

"I remember sitting in one."

It was rare for Caius to speak of his life, but the slaves who raised him had done it. He was hardly an object of pity, but for a moment Lela's heart was wrung. She could envision him, a lonely little boy whose parents cared nothing for him, sitting in the old stone sink at the Solstice House being attended by slaves. It did not surprise her that he remembered so far back. She knew the brilliance of his mind, but she thought she knew little of the pain in his soul.

She had stewed apples the previous night, mashing them and mixing them with honey. It was the one thing Anuska had eaten. Hopefully she would do it again, and hopefully Cauis would continue talking. Plopping the little one on her fat bottom in the dry, empty sink, Lela offered her apples on one of the child-sized spoons from the Hall. Eyes still pinned on Caius, the baby swallowed.

"Good," he said, beginning to move around their kitchen slowly, getting himself food. "Take care of her, I can help myself.

Make it happy for her."

Lela had not thought he knew a single thing about children, assuming he knew even less than she did. All at once she doubted her estimation and began to make it a game, smiling and chattering. She thought the baby's look of apprehension lessened somewhat, and she ate. Vaguely, Lela realized Caius was doing the same, which was a relief. She could not care for both of them at the same time.

"You have clean tunics," she nattered, torn between duties.

"I know. Just take care of the baby. She has been through a lot."

"So have you." She paused to let Anuska swallow.

But he just shrugged. "This was a feint. They saw something they wanted and came back to see how easily they might take it.

Which, unfortunately, was pretty easily."

"Then what can we do?"

"Roger already requested Earth troops. After the last incident, he knew they would be back. Apparently the colonies can call on each other for assistance, since they are closer than Earth. I assume he'll do that. They're going to come back."

"They always do." Lela had learned a lot during her short, brutal time as chattel to one of them. They came from a bandit planet torn by tribal feuds. When a clan had grown sufficiently numerous, though, they sometimes put together raiding parties to roam about looking for resources which, for them, were primarily minerals. They had mined their own planet bare of anything substantial, so they took their trade to other worlds, sometimes quietly abetted by those who would like to purchase their product below the common value. It was a subterranean business, abhorred by the organized colonies, who had armed against them. But Twelve was still vulnerable.

"We'll be getting reinforcements," Caius said, "and arms. We're going to have to run them off or suffer for it."

Lela knew exactly how they made women suffer.

* * * *

It was Dervin who laid their dead. There were twenty-one of them, Lela learned, citizens and guards alike. Most families had elected to keep their cremated remains individually, but the one thing all agreed upon was that there should be a Day of Memory.

They held it two days later in the silver

grass of the scarred city on a hilly knoll that served as a natural amphitheater. It was unthinkable not to attend and everyone did so, eight hundred people in serried ranks of gray. Because there was no one free to care for the children, they came, too—even little Anuska, dressed in a tiny gown Lela had hastily procured from the Hall and adorned with old-fashioned needle and thread stitches that her mother had shown her.

A middle-aged woman standing near them fingered it delicately before the solemnities began, smiling at the baby. "This is precious," she said. "Did you do it?"

"My mother taught it to me," Lela ventured. "I thought she should have something special for today."

Caius was looking fixedly ahead, at the ceremonial platform. She was on her own. But at least the baby was not screaming at his proximity. He had spent the night sleeping on their divan in the living quarters, leaving the bed for Lela and Anuska. Lela thought now it had been a wise precaution. The baby seemed somewhat more accepting of him in the daylight, surrounded by people.

"It's beautiful. I am Sinjal. My husband is helping above."

Lela had seen silhouettes of armed men on the higher ground. It was impossible to conceal a landing craft and they would know if anyone came. If anyone did, they would receive welcome at the point of laser cannon. She had seen those, too, trained on the landing site from atop buildings.

"I am—" Lela began, but the other woman nodded.

"We all know who you are," she said, not

unkindly. "And this is the Governor's niece, is she not?"

"She is." Lela stroked the baby's freshly-washed hair, ruffling in the breeze. It was a glorious day, too beautiful to commemorate death, yet there they were.

"It is terrible," Sinjal said. "I am so sorry for the families. We owe everything to those who died."

"And some who did not," Lela pointed out.

"Well, yes, of course. Your...err...he is not your husband, I think?" Lela nodded. "We know he fought admirably. We are grateful."

It was not the most tactful expression of thanks, but all things considered, Lela was happy to accept it. It might even be an overture; she was not certain. Most couples were married. Others had not yet made the commitment, but were bonded. It was frowned upon to have children, however, until vows had taken place. So Sinjal's inquiry could be censure, in part at least, or perhaps she was sincere. She need not have spoken at all, but Lela had a sudden suspicion that much was being overlooked because they now had an attachment to the Governor. He had entrusted a child of his family to them.

Below her, she saw young girls proceeding down the rows of mourners, passing each person a small plasticene goblet. Given one, she quickly ascertained by smell that it was spirits—the first she had seen on Twelve.

"Watch Dervin," Caius murmured beside her. "Do not drink until he does."

He would be accustomed to Earth customs, she realized, having served with

Earthers in the Mercenary Corps.

"There will be a toast," Sinjal confirmed from her other side. "Wait for it."

The baby was drowsing against her, lulled by the temperate sun and sweet breeze, as Dervin began to speak. It had been necessary to amplify his voice to reach all eight hundred, but it came through clearly.

Deliberately, he raised his goblet high into the air, and in unison all did the same.

"Hail!"

"Hail!" Echoed by eight hundred voices, resounding against the sides of the knoll, it made her skin shiver. It was recognizably a battle cry. Not such peaceful people after all. Caught in the emotion, Lela very nearly jumped when a hand descended on her shoulder from behind.

It was Roger, still so drawn and ashen she

understood why Dervin had substituted for him. He had come looking for his sister's child, she supposed.

"Something from our primitive past," he said, quaffing his spirits in a gulp. Everyone else was doing the same so Lela did it, too, though it made her eyes water. "We were not always as you see us now."

Lela regarded their Governor thoughtfully. Though the burden of responsibility made him seem older, he probably was not much older than Caius. He and his wife had not even been married long. He had no children of his own. How much more precious would his little niece be to him, then?

Finally, Caius turned from his own thoughts, re-engaging. "Your men remain good fighters."

"I know," Roger said, tight-lipped. "They need a good trainer. The job is yours, if you want it."

Caius merely nodded, touching his goblet to Roger's. Lela thought perhaps she was the only one who heard the faint note of irony in his reply.

"Of course."

Chapter Nine

There was a brief season of rain, customary on the temperate planet, but no sign of Dinovians. Lela watched the silver grass, the nonnis and the baby grow the same as Caius was doing.

Anuska no longer feared him, won over in part by being assured by her uncle that Caius was a friend and not a "bad man." He came to visit frequently and Lela, watching them together, knew it would not be long before he took her back. The baby loved him, calling him "Bawa," which they guessed was her version of Roger. She would babble to him incessantly, though not to anyone else. Whatever Bawa told her had great influence. Bawa just needed another wife or at least a good caretaker, Lela thought ruefully, and he would raise that child. They even looked something alike, blond and blue-eyed as many Earthers were. Anuska belonged with her own kind, but Lela wondered if she belonged anywhere.

People had been unmistakably kinder, which helped. Village mothers had sent her clothing for Anuska and the workers with whom she shared tasks included her in their gossip now. Life resumed a semblance of order, but beneath it, everyone was tense, waiting…waiting for any return of the Dinovians.

Instead, Earth soldiers arrived and immediately set about creating their own encampment. They were joined by small numbers of men and women from the eleven nearby planets that made up a loose confederacy with Twelve. They would rotate duty. All the planets were pledged to each others' defense because no one knew exactly what might threaten them from deep space. Most armament, however, still came from Earth, whose technology was acknowledged to be far superior to other races'.

To no one's surprise, Caius knew those weapons. Now he split his time between judgment, which was busier because of the presence of strangers who sometimes transgressed, and training. He had an easy camaraderie with the Earth soldiers, who recognized a similar soul despite outward appearances. He was a warrior. That, Lela thought, was precisely why they were on Twelve…why the Highest had sought to either control Caius or kill him. In an effete, corrupt society like Thelona's, a man like Caius was a real threat. On Twelve, he was a savior.

She should have been happy, but all her days were shadowed by the sense of impending loss. As she had foreseen, she loved the baby and would lose her. It was as she told Caius. What she loved, she lost.

* * * *

By the end of the rainy season, that became a reality. Once again, their self-effacing Governor simply walked to her house to tell her so. It was not far and she thought it was simply that Roger liked to walk. Beset all day by the problems of people, perhaps he found the time in their preserve restorative to his soul. He certainly needed that.

He came on a workday, not his usual time

to visit, so she understood immediately that he had wanted to find her alone. She wished Caius had been there, but he was not. He seldom was, too caught up in promulgating law and drilling men, appearing to think the fact that she had Anuska was enough to fulfill her. Seemingly, it did not occur to him that she felt empty inside without him. Even when they had moved the baby into a cot in a room of her own, he did not approach her for the wild sex that had been their habit. She missed it, not just for the physical release, but for the affirmation that he still loved her—that she was still important to him. Pouring love into an infant as she would, it was not enough.

And soon she would not even have that.

"Do you dislike transports?" she laughed, opening the door to Roger. She was easier with him as a result of his visits, seeing him not as the official who had admitted her to his planet but as a living, breathing human with problems and needs of his own. One of those needs was for the baby taking her mid-morning nap.

"Don't wake her," he said immediately. "I want to talk to you."

"Tea?" Lela tried to postpone the inevitable, but he shook his head.

"No, thank you. I wanted to suggest that I begin taking Anuska back to my dwelling. I have made the repairs there and found a friend to care for her."

"A friend?" Lela inquired with a gentle smile. One could not remain alone on Twelve for too long, if only because the work was so hard. Roger was still young enough to make another life. She should be glad for him.

"Perhaps more, eventually," he admitted. "I don't know. But I think she will be a stable person in Anuska's life and I would like for them to meet."

It was bound to happen. Lela stiffened her resolve, determined not to add to Roger's difficulties. He was beginning a new chapter in his life, as he should. "We will begin to wean her over to you, then."

"Not too quickly. She has grown to love you and I don't want to traumatize her."

"No." The torture would be prolonged, watching another woman take away her child. But that child was not hers to keep.

"Lela, I…need to know some things. Personal things. May I ask them of you?"

Suddenly she was wary. "What sort of things?"

"I want to try to help you," he clarified. "But there are things I need to know."

"Such as…

"How things stand with you and Caius."

"We are well enough."

"No, I mean really stand with you. Do you love him? Is he good to you?"

She contained her astonishment with an effort. "He is the best man I have known."

"That isn't what I asked." His gaze was penetrating. "I asked if you love him, if you plan to stay with him. You have never taken vows."

She already knew Caius would never feel himself bound by such strictures. "He has never asked, but yes."

"And he has never hurt you?"

"Hurt me? Good gods, no. What is this about?"

"When you were in stasis, the medicos made studies of you. It's a normal thing, to be sure the state is not harming you—done for everyone. You survived the trip well, but what they saw told them you had had fractures. And internal injuries. The kind that do not happen by themselves. We wondered…well, frankly, we wondered if he had done it."

She just shook her head. "Caius has never hurt me. He saved my life. He saved my…" She groped for the right word. "My being."

Roger was silent. She knew he wanted her to go on. There was a time when she had despised every man ever born but, like Caius, this one was different.

"My father sold me into slavery on Danaali. I don't know how well you know the place."

"Only that it is remote and still war-like."

"Yes. All sons old enough to fight go to war for their local chieftains, but the chieftains do not arm them. It would be too expensive.

Instead they let the families outfit them as best they can, so if there are girl children, poor families sell them when they mature to get the money."

"Ghastly," he said, but just the one word, without judgment of her. It allowed her to go on.

"I went to Thelona because girls with my coloring are much sought after there. An airco raped me almost the moment we arrived. One of the handlers there bought me cheap because I was damaged. He wasn't unkind, but it was just for the money and to bed me. He sold me to an old gentleman who was no threat, but I was pregnant."

Even to Roger she would not confess that she had killed her children rather than have them born into the life she had endured.

"I lost it. Old Lord Gorac died eventually

and his son sold me to one of the most venal of the Thelonian Lords. What went on in that House, you probably would not believe."

"One cannot do my work without seeing the worst, Lela. I would believe it."

She drew a deep breath. "He abused me unspeakably. For a season, he gave me to his nephew, who was just a boy. That one was kind; I almost thought I loved him. But his uncle was a pederast and that boy was his victim. I had never even known such things existed. Not all the Lords are like Caius. Some of them are the most contemptible creatures you can imagine."

"Then how did you come to Caius?"

"Not easily. I lost the child that boy got on me and they said I was worthless and sold me at Tyrenos. That is the worst of the slave markets, where only the defectives or the incorrigible go. I went to whore masters until they tired of me and sold me to a Dinovian."

Roger made a sound of pity and disgust.

"Yes, exactly. He beat me unmercifully first and last, especially when I lost still another child. Then I went back to the slave market in Syrstine, the capitol, and Caius found me."

She pulled at her hair nervously. "I don't know why he bought me—he was sorry for me, I suppose. He brought me back to health, he never forced me to do anything, and so I gave myself to him willingly. Now he has brought me here where I am free. So I will not leave him."

"You are a contradiction in terms, Lela," Roger commented. She had no idea what that was, but he didn't sound repulsed by what she had told him. "We knew you were hurt, but not how. I know you think you cannot have a child, but…"

"The midwife on Thelona told me I could not. She was very experienced."

"I'm sure," he said kindly. "But you are in another place now…a place where we have people even more experience."

"You mean there could be a chance?" It was a possibility so tantalizing, she dared not believe it, but she had seen these people do wonders. "I would like to give Caius a child of his own. He left his House, you see. It's imperative for a Lord of Thelona to have offspring, otherwise his House dies out. He cannot have that here, of course. The House of Bardin is gone forever. But I know it haunts him and I think he could bear it more easily if he had a son."

"Many men would feel so. Well, I cannot

promise you anything, Lela, I am not a medico. But we have managed to assist others who had difficulty conceiving their children. We have no birth chambers here, you would have to carry it, but it may be possible. I think it would be worth at least talking to someone. You needn't repeat what you told me here. That is between us. We will only tell them you need their help. That is, if Caius agrees. We do not do this unless both partners agree. And—" he sounded amused, "I think we will need his cooperation. Do you want me to ask him?"

She just nodded, unable to speak. Even to Caius she had never told so much of her life, if only to prevent him killing Lord Porlois, the worst of the lot. But she had seen Roger on the thin edge of losing his mind. They knew each other's deepest secrets now.

Chapter Ten

The city was more full than Lela had ever seen it. There were vehicles on the streets, since they were needed for repairs, and now there were others too. They came from off world with the people who accompanied them—uniformed Earth soldiers and volunteers from the other planets. The strangers were friendly, even respectful. But it was different. Twelve had changed.

The administrative center had changed, too. Some windows were still blown out and covered with thin blue film that cast a cerulean light on the usually gleaming white hallways. Lela suspected the medical suite was unchanged, though she had never been there. Such places still intimidated her and she would rather avoid them. But now she understood that she could not—not if she wanted a child.

Beside her, Caius squeezed her hand reassuringly and she remembered the way he had carried her from the medical quarters of the space transport. She wished he could do it again, but this was one time he could not help her. The fault for this lay with her and in the deadly poison she had taken to abort her other children. She knew they were better off, but it still troubled her.

"Here," he said, turning her to a large entry door. It opened for them at once and she stepped inside, into another world. A world of beeps, lights and machinery such as she remembered from the transport—only much larger. How would she bear it? But she had to.

They waited for entrance through another, much smaller door. This one led only to an office, clean and uncluttered compared to the organized chaos outside. A dark-haired woman, neither young nor old, stood and met with them a smile and a handshake.

"I am Dr. Patel," she introduced herself. An actual doctor, then, not a medico. Lela had never met one. "Please, make yourselves comfortable." She indicated two chairs— sumptuous and comfortable.

Caius made the introductions; Lela did not speak. To her consternation, the doctor pulled out a plasticene model. Lela just looked at it, puzzled. She had never seen anything like this.

"Lela, this is a model of what our studies showed. So that you can understand what troubles you." She pointed to a pear-shaped object. "This is a model of your uterus. Your womb," she clarified. "It is where you carry a child but not where you conceive it."

Lela glanced at Caius, wondering if he possibly knew these things. She thought he did, since he did not seem shocked in the least.

"This," and the doctor pointed to objects above the womb, "is where the egg that will form your child is made. And this…" she traced a line to the mock womb, "is the path the egg must travel to reach its destination. That is where the child is actually made, in the beginning…right about here." She put her finger on the in-between place. "It cannot happen for you because infection scarred your tubes. They are closed. Nothing can pass through, so no child can form."

"The midwife told me much the same," Lela admitted.

Dr. Patel nodded. "Very shrewd. Well, she was right."

"I was very ill with fever," Lela said.

"Yes, that is enough to do it. Now we must undo it."

"Can you?"

"Possibly." Lela sank back in her chair, disappointed. That was not a definite. But Roger had said there was no guarantee, she reminded herself.

"If we had all the resources of Earth at our disposal," the doctor went on, "we might be able to reverse the damage with advanced laser therapy." Lela hoped her face wouldn't betray the fact that she had no idea what that was.

"Unfortunately, we do not have that here, so we make do with other methods—older but often effective. We have the option of surgery to replace those tubes. It would be an invasive procedure."

"They would have to cut you," Caius clarified. He didn't sound pleased.

"Or," Dr. Patel added quickly, "there is another way."

And then she explained it to them, in detail, and Lela began to understand why Roger had sounded amused.

* * * *

They ate in one of the dining halls. People knew them now or at least, Lela corrected herself, they knew Caius. He was the one they recognized, and they no longer appeared half-afraid of him. But he did not linger for conversation. They took their food from the servers, and then he guided her to a small table in the back of the chamber where they could have more privacy.

"The gods, Caius," Lela said around bites of bio meat. Embarrassed or not, she was hungry. "Do you think I can really do this?"

"I think the question is more can I do it." She choked on her meat.

"Well, we all know *you* can do it," she said, recovering. "The only question is where."

"Oh, pretty much anywhere." She began to laugh.

"Are you going to help me with this or not?" she demanded, giggling.

"I am helping you. I can't wait to start, in fact."

She was laughing so hard she sensed people looking at them and recovered her dignity with an effort.

"You are bad, so bad," she chided him,

still red-faced.

Surprisingly, he reached over to take her hand. People were looking, and he was never demonstrative in public, but apparently this time he was going to be.

"Do you know," he asked, "there was a time when I never thought you would smile or laugh?"

"I remember." She coughed. "But you amused me."

"How fortunate."

She did remember. She remembered the misery of her life until he had taken her from it and taught her to smile again.

"Lela, it's completely up to you," he said. "You are the one who must go through the worst parts. And carry a child, and labor with it, and bear it. And then it is many years to raise it. I know you can do it. I saw you with

Anuska. But it will change everything for you, forever. So you should be sure."

"It will change everything for you, too," she pointed out.

"More for you, I think."

"Do you want a child?" she finally asked what she never had. "I assumed you did, but if not, say it."

"I think so," he said slowly. "I never really considered it. I was happy enough with the situation on Thelona. But things are different here. I think, though…well, the thought of you with my child inside you makes me want to put you on this table, right now."

* * * *

Caius had always been a prisoner of his instinct, Lela thought, and so had she. Rational thought had nothing to do with the way they made love and never had. It had been pure animal coupling from the outset. At one time, in fact, she had complained that she didn't like him even while craving him like a drug.

Now she lay drowsing with him in their bedchamber, feeling pleasantly ravaged. If he was going to be wasting his seed in a laboratory receptacle, she thought she wanted it one more time in the usual way. More often than not, he dominated her completely in the act, not even meaning to. It was his Thelonian nature. But she knew that he loved her and that, for him, it was the ultimate proof of that love. It was an even exchange, his strength and passion for her tenderness and nurture.

"Caius," she said quietly. "I love you."

It was the first time she had ever said it. He rolled over, reaching to twine his hands in her hair, to look into her face.

"I have always loved you," he said, simply. "Always."

"Why?" He had bought her, like a plaything. But even then, after years of men abusing her, she had known he was different. Was it love that she had sensed? Was that why she had finally given herself to him with a whole heart?

"Because you're brave," he said. "You are the bravest woman I have ever known. I wasn't sure I wanted children, but yes, I do—if they are yours."

"A slave's children?"

"You are no slave." He laughed, shortly. "You never were. You were my match right from the start, remember? I told you someone would beat your brains out one day and that would be the end of you—because they were making a slave of a woman who wasn't." His fingers traced the sides of her face, delicately, as if framing it. "How did you get that way?"

"I told my family they had no honor, selling me. If they did not have it, I would."

"And you did." He pulled her down, kissing her gently now—neck, shoulder, breast, belly. It was nothing but pure sensation, all for her pleasure. It was how she liked him best. She moaned, opening her legs, offering herself again. He took her quickly and urgently, arms around her, pulling her against him. The power of speech completely left her; she just held him to her and let herself be loved.

Chapter Eleven

It was hard. Painful. Tedious. Humiliating, too, despite the kindness of the doctors. But by the next rainy season, Lela was seven months pregnant. The fourth child she had conceived would be the one who came to fruition—safe, wanted and free.

Virtually the entire medical department had exulted with them when a viable pregnancy was confirmed. They always did, of course, but Lela sensed they knew this one had been special. So special, so unimaginable. She knew then that she would have endured anything for the son she carried. Everything she had gone through—all the suffering, the hardship, the degradation—would all have been worth it for this one thing.

Then the Dinovians came.

* * * *

All their communicators went off at once. All over the preserve, a shrill cacophony of beeping traveled on the night air like a million song-bugs.

Caius sat bolt upright beside her in bed.

"All right, you know what to do," he said.

"Oh, no, it can't be," she protested.

"It probably is."

There was not much she could say to that. The amount of men and materials pouring in from Earth had been truly impressive, especially considering that they were defending a colony of only 1,200 people. But there was a reason for that and it was likely the Dinovians knew it, too. Precious minerals long since exhausted on earth had been discovered on its last, fledgling colony. Twelve had assumed an importance, and a vulnerability, it had never wanted. But Earth and the other colonies had been dutifully shoring up their defenses. There was nowhere an unscheduled ship could descend that it would not be detected.

Caius scanned the text on his communicator quickly. "Multiple ships," he said. "I have to go."

Terror leapt into her throat, real and stifling, but at least it kept her from weeping and begging. She had been afraid she might, if it ever came, but now the moment had arrived and she could not.

"Go to the Hall," Caius said, kissing her briefly. "Be careful."

"You be careful."

Then he left her, seven months pregnant and terrified. But all the men would be doing the same thing, she told herself.

Outside, she could hear transports, running footsteps and people shouting. Sliding into sturdy shoes that her increasing bulk demanded, which should help keep her from falling in the dark, she went outside. She paused only to retrieve a torch and a tactical from the storage unit, now kept unlocked since Anuska had returned to her uncle.

"Lela!" someone called. "Wait, we will take you." Scurrying footsteps announced the arrival of two of the girls she worked with in the goat pens, not that she had been there much lately. But they had remembered and she was grateful.

"Come on," Doris, the little red-haired

girl, hooked her tactical over her shoulder so that she could take Lela's left arm while, while Mandra grabbed the right. "We'll take you up."

Lela could still move well, but the company helped keep her from panic. With her tactical bumping against her hip, she went up the incline to the Hall where all the other women were streaming in. Every one of them was armed.

Transports were lifting. She couldn't begin to guess which one Caius was on or when he would return, or if he would return, and as she had nearly reached the Hall she saw those in the doorway turn, staring in unison at the sky.

The Dinovian ships had not made for the landing site, where they could be shot down from the ground, but were discharging their cargo within easy sight of the preserve.

Hovering above the empty fields, they simply opened hatches and threw lines on which Dinovians began to descend. It looked like they were under attack by a horde of alien spiders. For the first time, Lela thought she was probably going to die. Refuge in the Hall, armed with tacticals, was never going to save them.

Abruptly, their departing transports turned in mid-air. They had been armed and cannon fire erupted. The hovering craft, probably rogue ships hired for a price, were no match for them. Their intent seemed to be to drop as many men as possible before trying to escape. Lela and the other women could see lines of fire shuddering along the seams of the ships as lasers cut those not fast enough to ascend. Some simply dropped their lines of Dinovians, shedding them like something cast off, and now the women had work.

"Stay here!" Doris gasped, then she and Mandra joined the others running down the hill past animal pens to the pastures where Dinovians would have to get through the force fences. They were empty of animals, which had been taken in for the night, and those fences had been turned up to lethal charge by some alert sentry. Lela could hear the screams of men who hit them unawares and the simultaneous thrum of tactical weapons discharging. In the absence of their men, the women swept fire side to side from outside the fence, as they had been instructed to do in the event of a raid. Fingers of light from their scopes spread a deadly pattern across the pastures, illuminating figures of running men— no, demons, Lela thought. She would not risk herself running down to that field, but stood at the top with her tactical aimed to take individual shots. She had the high ground and Caius had trained her well.

More of the alien craft split off, turning in the direction of Capitol. Lela clutched her belly, aware for the first time of cloying ozone in the air—the residue of heavy weapons fire borne by the wind, rolling uphill towards the Hall. This could not be good for the baby, she thought, and ran inside to escape it.

"Turn off the fence," someone screamed, and she hit the panel inside the door, hard, even as she wondered why. By the light of their scopes, she could see the women now running downhill into the pastures where they worked, which they knew by heart, in pursuit of Dinovians who, unwilling to take further losses, were heading in the direction of the mines. They would be surprised by what they found there.

The women began to return, since the Dinovians could outrun them. They had taken down as many as they could. Lela's two guardians returned unscathed. "Are you all right?" Mandra demanded, clearly alarmed that Lela was breathing hard and sheltering her belly.

"Just…the ozone," Lela managed to gasp. Then darkness enveloped her.

* * * *

The beeping was annoying and puzzling. For a moment she was totally confused. Was it the beep of equipment in the medical bay of the transport? The beeping of communicators? She couldn't discern it, but then as she had heard him in the transport, she heard Caius again.

"It's all right, Lela, be still."

He had told her that before, she thought, wincing. Something hurt. Coming out of stasis didn't hurt. Something was wrong, so she opened her eyes.

She was in the medical bay, but not the transports. This was in the city. Her field of vision cleared and in the bluish light of the bay she saw Caius and Dr. Patel and numerous other doctors and medicos. Large portable scoping machines were rolling above her, mapping every inch of her body. She tried to feel for her belly, but her arms were strapped down.

"Hold very still," Caius said. "Don't move, they're scoping you. You took a good shot of ozone. Knocked you out. They want to be sure the baby is all right."

So, she had not lost it, at least. That was

her first, most primal fear, but then the analytical part of her mind told her the danger was not yet over. If she had breathed ozone, so had her baby. He might very well be damaged, even dead. She felt the slow leak of tears from her eyes and then Caius's big hand on her face, wiping the tears.

"Don't," he whispered. "Don't cry. They are going to take very good care of you."

Good care would avail her nothing if the baby was poisoned. Poisoned...

"Gods, no!" she gasped. "Caius, you don't know. You don't know!"

"What don't I know?"

"There were three."

"Three what?"

"Babies! I slipped three babies. Not just the one you knew about. I poisoned them, so they would not be slaves."

Above her she saw Caius move quickly, blocking out her view of the medicos hovering above her. Their studiously blank expressions told her they had overheard, but this should be a private conversation. Caius bent over, speaking only for her.

"I knew you took the bane. Remember when I took it from you? I didn't want you to kill yourself."

"I should have," she moaned. "I should. I'm paying for it now. Oh, Caius, you don't deserve this."

"You don't either," he said. "The gods are not judging you and neither am I."

"But Dinovians..." she faltered. "That was the last one. From a Dinovian."

"I should have killed more of them."

"Are they gone?" She felt herself slipping back into the abyss. If the gods wanted her life, they could have it, but not her baby. Please, not him.

"Yes," Caius said—the last word she heard.

Chapter Twelve

She thought the beeping would drive her mad, or perhaps she already was—that, and the fact that she was still restrained. But she appeared to be no longer in the bay. She lay in a medical bed in a small room with a window and a view of the city. It was daylight. They had gotten through the night or perhaps many nights. Her sense of time was gone.

She whimpered and heard a stir by the wall, then a stronger, summoning beep. Caius came into sight and she gave him a wan smile, telling him she was still alive. He looked as if he hadn't slept in a month.

"How do you feel?" he asked the age-old

question to the ill and injured. She thought she was both. There was a pain in her belly like a beast had clawed it.

"Awful." Her mouth was dry as dust. "What happened?"

Behind him, Dr. Patel was coming in the door and answered. "The baby wasn't doing well, so we took him. He is in our nursery, doing better now."

"It's too soon," Lela whispered, choking. Like most humanoids, she needed to carry nine months or more. Caius cupped the back of her head to lift it and held a plasticene cup to her lips. It was water. She gulped thankfully.

"Seven months is not ideal, no," the doctor admitted. "And, unfortunately, we don't have a birth chamber where we could keep him as if he was still in the womb. Those are on Earth, not here, and he is too critical to transport. But we can support him and fortunately he is a good weight." She smiled at Caius. "I believe he takes a great deal from you. That will work in his favor."

"When you are able to walk, we will take you to see him," the doctor said, unstrapping her arms. "But you should be quiet right now. Do you feel like you could eat?"

Food had been the last thing on Lela's mind, until then. "Yes."

"Just liquids at first," Dr. Patel cautioned, and Lela made a wry face. It was like coming out of stasis—no real food.

"We will get you something," the doctor promised and walked out the door to get it herself—not something doctors did.

"You look so tired," she said to Caius. She didn't ask if he had been with her the whole time. When he had promised that he would never leave her—it seemed like eons ago—he had meant it.

"I am all right," he said. Reaching down, he gently stroked back her silky hair that he had always loved for its color and its difference from his. "He has your hair, at least so far."

She smiled. She didn't care if the baby had red frizz, as she had expected. "Did you name him? If he is to go to the gods, he should have a name."

"He is not going to the gods," Caius said firmly. "I thought, if you liked it, we could call him Antin."

Antin, alone of all the Lords on Thelona, had helped engineer their escape from the planet and they had never known his fate. They owed Verulia's husband their lives. "It is a good name."

"He will live," Caius insisted again. "And

you will live and we will be whole again. I promise you."

No one could promise the judgment of the gods, she thought, but let Caius believe it if it pleased him. He would anyway.

* * * *

She stayed six days in the medical bay until they considered her well enough to go home. The baby could not leave, Dr. Patel told them, not yet. Lela had seen him every day, tiny and helpless, nearly obscured by equipment as he lay in a clear plasticene bubble. She had not been able to touch or comfort him, and neither could Caius. All they could do was wait and hope. She felt torn in half to leave him, but she was not recovering well enough herself. Constantly disturbed by lights and noises and worry, she barely slept, and the pain she endured was as bad as any beating she had ever received. She needed to go home.

They had cut the baby out of her. It was exactly the fate she had been promised by the Dinovian who had impregnated her, but in that case, it was meant to kill her. She had always thought it would. Apparently, the Earth-trained physicians did not kill their patients, but it still was not easy.

"I have brought you one of your old gowns," Caius explained, coming to take her home. "You will not be able to wear trousers for a long time, I think. These will do."

Lela no longer cared if she scandalized the entire colony with her attire from Thelona. The binder she wore beneath the sheer top to prevent milk leaking onto it made her presentable, in her opinion, and the loose skirt did not rub her painfully swollen and tender belly. It was all she cared about at that moment.

"It's one of my favorites," she said, letting Caius know it was all right.

"Good." He helped her change into it, playing lady's maid. She remembered that he had done it at Cas Solar, though then it had been for purposes of seduction. Now it was simply to get her home.

"Roger sent a transport," he said. "We have a new bed and some other things to make you comfortable."

"Oh, that's nice." Again, she really didn't care. "Caius, how can we leave him here?"

"How can we not?" he asked, so reasonably that she wanted to hit him. "He will have the best of care and you can get some rest.

You know you are not resting here. You need to be home."

"I need my son." Although everyone had assured her Antin was a beautiful baby, with Caius's golden skin and her dark hair, all she saw when she looked at him was his fragility.

"You must rest," Caius repeated stubbornly. "Now will you come or must I carry you?"

He would do it. He had done it before. So she went with him, shuffling painfully down the hallways that now seemed interminable. They were lined with well-wishers, but she was too distraught and in too much pain to take much notice. Once they got to the transport, he did have to pick her up. She couldn't get in unassisted. He carried her like a child from the place where she had given birth.

It was a glorious, sunny day bursting with

the promise that always accompanied the end of the rainy season. Native wildflowers and plants imported from Earth spread a colored carpet beneath them as the transport skimmed low to the ground for the short trip. Lela began to feel a faint interest despite herself. The medical bay had practically driven her mad. It had been as if the outer world had disappeared. Now it lay in promise beneath them. This would be her son's world, if he survived.

Their pilot circled the village to the north, uphill, where she could see their little house. But then he kept flying.

"Where are you going?" she asked, but he just gave her a cheeky grin. "Caius? Where are we going?"

"Home. They have given us new quarters now that we have Antin. We need more room."

Well, that was true. Caring for Anuska in

their limited quarters had been difficult. The pilot adroitly circled the southern boundary that housed families with children and then set down virtually in the yard of a neat square white house with a red-tiled roof. Shrubs and flowers framed the door, which was also red, and she could see old-fashioned curtains through the windows. She was touched. Caius knew she still preferred them.

"Many thanks," Caius told their pilot, who wished her well and began to engage his flight gear. He would not linger, apparently, so she let Caius lift her out again, steadying her on the hard-packed earth.

"It's nice," she said. "Bigger, anyway."

"Quite a bit," he agreed. "You will like it."

There was no sound except for the droning of a few insects cruising among the flowers. Perhaps this would be a peaceful place where she could regain her strength. Then Caius opened the door.

"Surprise!" She nearly recoiled at the welcome, shouted by more people than she had seen since the Day of Memory. They were packed into her new house, every one of them hiding inside. There was a roar of laughter at her stunned expression and she felt Caius's knee firmly planted in her butt to prevent her from backing out.

All of their old furniture had been moved to the new house, with additions. There were curtains, there were couches and reclining chairs, even scattered rugs. Glowlights, a view screen over a hearth that looked as if real wood could be burned in it. A gorgeous electronic mural showing mountains such as she had seen on Danaali. It looked as if she could walk right into it and be in her old home again.

Then there were the people. Across her living room she saw Roger with Anuska and his new partner. He looked more relaxed and happy than she had seen him in ages. Dervin was there with his wife and tribe of offspring, all ginger-haired like their father. It looked as if he was populating Twelve single-handed. Sinjal was there, the woman who had befriended her at the Day of Memory, with her husband who had stood guard. Simla, matron at the Hall, and the two girls from the goat pen were there—Lois and Mandra—and others she did not know as well. The captain of the Guard. Two medicos who apparently were not on duty. Various other people she'd never seen in her life. Everyone had come.

It reminded her of the night Caius had insisted that she, a slave, dine with his patrician friends. She had been terrified and sure they would reject her out of hand, yet those had turned out to be the people who had saved their lives. These people had brought food, they had brought gifts. They inundated her with joyous celebration and an unmistakable air of triumph. Successful in defending their colony with few losses, blessed with a new member, they were in the mood to celebrate. Dazzled and aching, finally she let Caius lower her carefully into a chair so voluptuous she knew he would have to pull her out again. She would never be able to get up unassisted but she didn't have to. People brought her everything she needed and along with it their friendship.

Roger and his friend were last to approach. She was a pretty girl with long reddish hair and unusual green eyes—a stunner. But her smile was warm and real as she walked with Anuska across the crowded room.

"Baby!" Lela greeted her as the superannuated toddler made a direct line across the floor to her at top speed.

"Lela, this is Nica," Roger introduced his companion as the baby tried to climb on top of Lela, babbling in her private language punctuated with clearly understood phrases—new words. She was not the quiet, withdrawn child she had been. Lela was stricken all over again by longing, wondering if her own child would live to fulfill such potential. After all, as she had told Caius, she always lost what she loved.

It would be hard to lose all the love in that room, though, overflowing and embracing her. It might even be enough to let her finally come home.

Chapter Thirteen

On the nineteenth day, they could finally have their child.

Lela had visited faithfully every day, Caius less often as the demands of his accumulated work piled up, but when he did, his expression of wonder was so profound that there were no words for it. How did you really explain such a thing?

Little by little, she had been able to touch her baby, talk to him, stroke him, then eventually to hold him. She thought him beautiful, even though she knew every other mother felt the same about their child. None of them had one like Antin. He appeared destined to be a perfect amalgam of herself and Caius. The medicos had been amazed that his eyes were not blue—not at any time. Lela's were the clear blue of a crystal lake and they told her that was typical of Earth's newborn children, but Antin had his father's eyes. He was the color of the oatmeal cookies she had begun to enjoy, with an underlying rosiness he got from her. He delighted her.

They took him home on a small shuttle transport, his first flight but undoubtedly not his last. Twelve seemed to be growing right before her eyes. This child would fly. He would do many things she had never dreamed of.

She refused to put him in any sort of carrier going home but took him in a cloth sling that looped around her neck, holding him next to her heart. She rested her head on

Caius's arm behind her, circling both of them.

"I hope he looks like you," she said.

His arm tightened around her, infinitesimally, and he gave her a small, conspiratorial smile.

"Caius, tell me the truth. Is he going to be safe here?"

"As safe as anywhere," he replied, "and better than most. The Dinovians never expected what they got here last time. I don't think they'll come back in a hurry. The only real threat is if they stop fighting each other and assemble a fleet, but if they do that, I think Earth will annihilate them."

"They would do that?"

"If they had to."

She shook her head, puzzled yet again by Earthers. Such open, friendly people with so much knowledge it boggled her simple mind and yet, if you gave them cause, they would kill you just like any of the primitive species. She no longer underestimated them. "Here we stand and here we stay," was their motto. She had heard it first from Dervin, on the Day of Memory. It was not the last time, though.

Sighing, she rested. For the first time that she could remember, she felt fully at peace, and she thought there was something more settled and satisfied about Caius as well. In part it was the baby, in part it was their new home, and in large measure it was the fact that he was needed. There was no doubt they would have a standing army now. Their time of innocence was past. Roger might have the final authority over it, but men like Caius would be its backbone. He was above all a protector and it was where he belonged.

"Do you ever dream of Thelona?" she

asked.

He looked startled. "Very seldom. Why? Do you?"

"Sometimes. I think it comes in dreams because it seems less and less real to me. But, of course, I was there only eight years."

"Well, I was there my whole life," Caius reflected, "except for the years in the Corps and I always knew I would leave." He paused for a moment, then spoke resolutely.

"I told you when I first met you that the aircos would strip us of resources and then leave us fighting for scraps. I am sure that's just what they did. Trying to depose one petty ruler would have meant nothing but more misery for the people."

"You have not tried to find out?"

"No."

It was a telling statement. He had truly

cut his ties—all of them. That would be like leaving a lover, she thought, never knowing what happened to them. It was just what he had done. Verulia had never quite admitted having slept with Caius, but Lela knew she had. They had both been young, but he was locked in a conflict with his parents to which he responded by going off planet. He had left her, so Verulia—titled and patrician—did the expected thing and married a man of her class who could give her the things that were expected. But she had always been half in love with Caius. That was why she had sent her husband to help save them and why he had done it. Antin had risked his life, his home and his fortune to try to win the love of his wife. She wondered if Caius knew. She didn't think so. It took a woman to understand some things.

"You do not think of going back now?"

she questioned.

"No. No, Lela, that is past. There is nothing to return to. My mother is surely dead by now. She was old when we left. Our friends are older or dead, too, if they stood in opposition to the Highest. And the aircos will continue plundering everything of value while it lasts, then disappear into the stars. There is nothing for us on Thelona. There never was."

She could love it at least a little, Lela thought, for the memory of the one summer at Cas Solar—the summer she had admitted, if only to herself, that she loved Caius.

"You were too good for Thelona," she said.

"As you were."

Their flight was coming to an end, but Roger had made it clear that a transport was at her disposal at any time. Partly it was his thanks for taking in his niece, partly it was out of respect for Caius. But mainly it was because he was a good man. She had known the most brutal of men. But she had also known the best of them.

They went in past their pretty flowers, into their home furnished by the hands of friends. She thought there was one thing left to say to Caius and then she would let the past be the past, forever.

"I am only sorry," she said, "for the fall of your House."

Turning, he kissed her gently on the forehead—not the kiss of passion but the kiss of tenderness. With one hand, he cupped the baby's tiny head, nestled against her.

"It didn't fall," he replied, "it's right here. You are my House."

THE END

About the Author:

Fantasy poetry driven by myths and legends has been my passion for as long as I can remember. I was published in poetry before catching the romance writing bug. I bring that background to my writing along with a lifelong addiction to horses, an 18 year career in various areas of psychiatric social services and many trips to Ireland, where I nurture my muse. My published works range from contemporary fantasy romance to fantasy historical, futuristic, science fiction and historical romance. Currently I live in rural Pennsylvania with a "motley crew" of rescue animals. You can see my books at www.miriamnewman.com.

You can connect with Miriam at:
Blog: www.thecelticroseblog.blogspot.com
Facebook:
https://www.facebook.com/AuthorMiriamNewman/

Other Books By Miriam Newman:

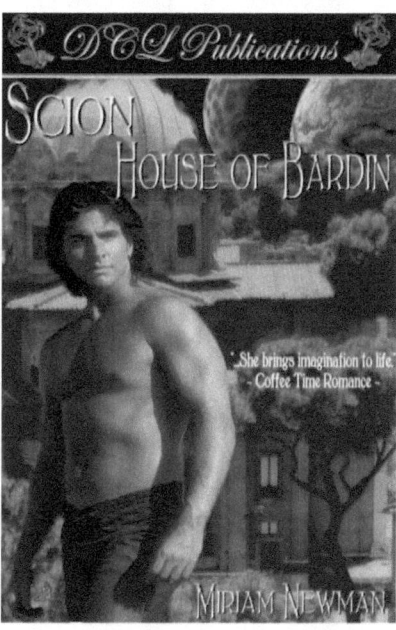

Scion
House of Bardin
Book I

After eight years as a rebellious sex slave on the planet Thelona, Lela is weary and jaded. When she is purchased in the public square by a bored aristocrat, she only hopes he will tire of her and let her go to work in his kitchens. Caius, forced into the lifestyle of the idle rich by his return to Thelona after eight years in the Mercenary Corps, thinks he has only bought a night's pleasure. Two restless kindred spirits who won't be tamed never expect what happens next.

Scion
House of Ruin
Book II

When the beleaguered citizens of the capitol city of Thelona are swept by plague in the absence of their ruling class, who have fled it en masse, desperation finally pushes them to take to the streets. With their city burning, the Lords of Thelona have no choice but to shoulder the burden of responsibility. In the absence of their Highest, they turn to Caius, Scion of the House of Bardin. He has unwittingly placed himself in the path of his ruler's ambitions and also endangered his human slave, Lela. What will become of the House of Bardin?

The Eagle's Woman

Son of an impoverished, dying Norse chieftain, Ari raids for booty and slaves so he can feed his people. Pagan himself, still he spares priests though he sells them. He's a heathen, a murderer, and it is a sin for any Christian woman to love him. Yet when he abducts Maeve from her peaceful Irish fishing village, he may have found the one woman who can.

Stupid Cupid

When the son of Zeus and Aphrodite bumbles into a meadow south of Killarney, he is met by a band of indignant faeries outraged by his target practice. Soon, however, all the supernatural creatures are overshadowed by an estranged couple intent on fisticuffs! Can Cupid effect a reconciliation between the humans? Or is just a wee bit of intervention by the Fae in order?

The Comet

An ambitious young Norman knight, Neel, is seriously wounded at the Battle of Hastings and nursed back to health by a Saxon girl, Rowena. For her, it is only a matter of Christian duty and she is shocked to receive his proposal of marriage in return. She dares not refuse, but how can she love a Norman?

The Chronicles of Alcinia

Available for the first time as an e-book bundle, the award-winning fantasy historical series The Chronicles of Alcinia weaves a tale of war, history, passion and romance. In Book I, The King's Daughter, Tarabenthia of Alcinia should grow to inherit her father's throne by the rocky cliffs of the sea. When invaders seize her land, what will she sacrifice in the name of love? In Book II, Heart of the Earth, the Northern Prince who has always wanted Tia saves her life. But will the price of his protection be too high? And finally in Book III, Ice Maiden, readers who wondered about the fate of Tia's oldest son have their answer. Sometimes heart-wrenching, always powerful, this is a tale of heroes and the women who love them.

Spirit Awakened

In a pre-medieval land recently torn by war, a woman with no voice and no memories struggles to survive. Drawn by need to a small farm, she encounters a man equally in need, though for different reasons. They are each other's only hope, and the future for their land. In a time of spiritual awakening, can they and their country survive? Or will the twin enemies of fear and persecution triumph?

Invanine

He was her slave in one land, her lover in another. When the king's sister saves a rebel from a troubled province, her act of mercy changes her life irrevocably and influences the course of her country's future.

www.ingramcontent.com/pod-product-compliance
Lightning Source LLC
Chambersburg PA
CBHW022126170626
46808CB00002B/866